RESISTANCE

BY A. JUNGMAN

illustrated by
Alan Marks

Librarian Reviewer
Kathleen Baxter
Children's Literature Consultant, formerly with Anoka County Library, MN
BA College of Saint Catherine, St. Paul, MN
MA in Library Science, University of Minnesota, MN

Reading Consultant
Elizabeth Stedem
Educator/Consultant, Colorado Springs, CO
MA in Elementary Education, University of Denver, CO

 STONE ARCH BOOKS
Minneapolis   San Diego

First published in the United States in 2006
by Stone Arch Books,
151 Good Counsel Drive, P.O. Box 669,
Mankato, Minnesota 56002.
www.stonearchbooks.com

Published by arrangement with
Barrington Stoke Ltd, Edinburgh.

Library of Congress Cataloging-in-Publication Data
Jungman, Ann.
    Resistance / by Ann Jungman; illustrated by Alan Marks.
    p. cm. — (Pathway Books)
    Summary: In the occupied Netherlands during World War II, Jan and
Elli are ashamed that their fathers work for the Nazis, and they try to find a
way to help the Dutch underground resistance.
    ISBN-13: 978-1-59889-001-3 (hardcover)
    ISBN-10: 1-59889-001-8 (hardcover)
    ISBN-13: 978-1-59889-198-0 (paperback)
    ISBN-10: 1-59889-198-7 (paperback)
    1. World War, 1939–1945—Netherlands—Juvenile fiction. [1. World
War, 1939–1945—Netherlands—Fiction. 2. Netherlands—History—German
occupation, 1940–1945—Fiction. 3. World War, 1939–1945—Underground
movements—Netherlands—Fiction. 4. Friendship—Fiction.] I. Marks, Alan,
1957– ill. II. Title. III. Series.
PZ7.J957Res 2006
[Fic]—dc22   2005026576

1 2 3 4 5 6 11 10 09 08 07 06

Printed in the United States of America.

TABLE OF CONTENTS

4

CHAPTER 1

MAJOR KONRAD

"Checkmate," said Major Konrad. "I've beaten you at chess again, Bakker. You need to think about what you are doing."

"I could never beat you at chess, Major. You are too good for me," said Mr. Bakker. "You could be a world grandmaster if there wasn't a war going on."

This made Jan Bakker angry.

He had been watching his father and the major finish their game. He knew that his father could beat the German officer any time. But his dad just let Major Konrad win.

Jan knew why his father did this. The Bakkers were Dutch, and the Germans had invaded Holland. Jan's father worked for the Germans. He was in the Nazi Police. The major could help them. It was worth being nice.

Jan's mother slammed the kettle down on the stove. She was angry, too.

"Are you making coffee, Mrs. Bakker?" asked Major Konrad.

"Yes," she said. "But not real coffee. This is the awful stuff we Dutch have to drink."

"It's made from acorns and things," she added. "Would you like a cup?"

"Ah, but I have something for you," he said with a smile.

I hate having this Nazi in our house!

The major pulled a small package from his pocket. "Some real coffee as a gift from the German government."

Jan's mother took the package. She said nothing. Soon the room was full of the rich smell of real coffee. Jan longed for some. His mother took the boiling kettle off the stove and went to get cups from the shelf. She only got two.

"Aren't you having any, Mrs. Bakker?" asked Major Konrad.

"No, Major, it will only keep me awake. Now off to bed, Jan, you have school tomorrow."

"But, Mother," said Jan, as she pushed him out of the kitchen. "I love coffee, you know I do. And so do you."

"No one else in Holland is drinking real coffee just now. We can do without it, too," she told him. There was anger in her voice. "Now go to bed." She gave him a kiss.

Jan lay in his bed and shivered. It was cold outside, and there was very little coal to heat the house. I wish all this was over, he thought. I wish the Germans would get out of Holland, so things could get back to normal. He remembered how much fun life had been before the war and smiled.

Outside he could hear Major Konrad leaving. Jan looked out.

"Heil Hitler!" cried Major Konrad, raising his arm in the Nazi salute.

"Heil Hitler!" replied Jan's father and raised his arm.

Jan looked across the street and saw people watching from their windows. He crawled back into bed. Even when this awful war is over, he thought, it won't be over for us. Everyone hates us.

It was like this all the time. Jan wished his father wasn't helping the Germans.

CHAPTER 2

SCHOOL

"Jan!" shouted his mother. "Hurry up. You know how angry Miss Hals gets if you're late for school."

Jan picked up his bag, but he didn't hurry. School was terrible these days. He set off sadly down the road, walking very slowly.

Jan waited for something bad to happen. It didn't take long. A boy in his class, Pieter, came up beside him.

"And how did you enjoy your real coffee last night?" he asked.

"I didn't drink any coffee," Jan told him.

Another boy, Willem, came up on the other side of Jan. "Oh, so it was just Mommy and Daddy drinking coffee with the nice German officer, was it?" he mocked.

Then Willem grabbed Jan's bag and tossed it over a fence. The three boys watched the bag as it flew through the air and landed near a canal.

"Why are you doing this? You used to be my friends," said Jan.

"That was before your dad started helping the Germans. Before my dad was sent away to a work camp in Germany," said Willem.

"Too bad your bag didn't fall into the canal," said Pieter. "Then Miss Hals would have been really angry."

Jan climbed over the fence and picked up his bag. I'll be late for school again, he thought. But he didn't mind.

He hated school these days.

No one spoke to him. It was worse now that some of the children's fathers had been taken away. No one knew if they were alive or dead. That was why the other children hated Jan so much. His father was not going to be sent to Germany.

* * *

Just as Jan got to school, the town clock struck eight.

"Late again, Jan Bakker," said Miss Hals angrily. "Third time in a week. You will have to stay after school and clean up as a punishment."

"It won't be so bad," she added. "You'll have a nice, hot cup of real coffee waiting for you when you get home."

"Mother and I didn't drink any of that coffee," Jan told her angrily. "Mom says if no one else in Holland can have coffee, then we won't drink it either."

"I see," said Miss Hals. "Well, well. You will have to stay after school anyway. You've been late too often."

Jan sat at the back of the room as he always did.

No one spoke to him. No one looked at him. It was as if he wasn't there.

Then the door opened, and Elli Wessel came in. Her eyes were red.

It was a surprise to see her at all.

Elli hardly ever came to school. She was always out sick.

Is it because her father, like my father, is in the Nazi Police? thought Jan. She was bullied by the other children, too.

As Elli walked through the class to the back of the room, all the others looked down at their desks, as if she wasn't there.

Elli sat down next to Jan. He put his hand on her arm.

Elli smiled at him, dried her eyes, and wrote him a note:

> *I can't stand the silence any more.*
> *No one will talk to me.*

Jan wrote back:

> *I know. I feel the same way, but be brave.*
> *We haven't done anything wrong,*
> *and the war will be over soon.*

Elli wrote back:

> *It will never be over for us.*
> *People will never forgive anyone*
> *who was on the side of the Nazis.*

"What's this?" Miss Hals was standing over them. "You two have been writing notes to each other?"

She grabbed the paper and read it.

"Oh dear," she said sadly. "Your fathers help the Nazis, and you pay the price. The rest of us don't understand how hard it must be for you, Jan and Elli."

CHAPTER 3

STRIKE

After school, Jan followed Elli out of the building. "Do you want me to walk home with you?" he asked.

"Why?" she asked.

"To make sure you get home safely. And so you'll have someone to talk to."

"It's awful, isn't it?" said Elli. "By not speaking to us, the other children tell us how much they hate us."

When Jan got home, his father was banging his fist on the table and shouting at his mother. "They're crazy, I tell you. They're crazy! No good will come of this."

"What's wrong?" asked Jan.

"All the railway men are going to strike. The trains won't run at all in Holland," said his father.

"Why?" asked Jan.

"So the Germans can't move men and guns around."

"What will happen to the railway men?" asked Jan.

"They'll be sent to prison," his father told him. "And the leaders may be shot."

"What else will the Germans do?" asked Jan.

"They are going to cut off all our coal and food," said his mother. "It will be a long, hard winter. We won't have heat or light, and there will be very little food."

"What will we do?" Jan asked.

"We'll have to get wood from the forests and food anywhere we can," his mother told him. "The farmers won't give us any food. Everyone knows that your father is on the side of the Nazis. It's going to be a very hard winter for us unless the major brings us more of his presents."

CHAPTER 4

IN THE WOODS

It got harder and harder to find food to eat or wood for a fire. Everyone was hungry and cold. At school, the children wore all the clothes they had. The older boys were gone. Some had been sent to work in Germany. Others were in hiding.

Every day and night, British and American planes flew over the town on their way to bomb Germany.

"The war will be over soon," Jan said to Elli one day when they were looking for wood in the forest.

"My mother listens to the London radio. They say the Americans and the British have landed in France. They'll be here soon," she told him.

"It's a crime to listen to the London radio," Jan said. "Be careful."

"The Germans don't worry about our families," Elli told him. "After all, our fathers have joined the Nazi Police."

"So that makes you and me Nazi-lovers, too?" asked Jan.

"Does it?" said Elli. She turned and looked at him hard. "Do you want the Germans to win this war?"

"They bomb our towns," said Elli. "They take away our men and our food. They put anyone who is against them in prison or shoot them. How do you feel, Jan?"

Jan was thinking hard. "You're right, Elli. I hate the Germans. Our fathers made a stupid and wicked choice. They joined the Nazis. That doesn't mean we have to do the same thing, does it?"

"No, Jan, but what can we do about it?"

"Nothing," said Jan sadly. "The Dutch Resistance would not let us join them. They'd think we might betray them to the Germans."

"That's right," agreed Elli, "but we can fight the Nazis in our own way."

"What do you mean?" asked Jan. "I don't understand."

"Just think a moment," said Elli. "Which children in our class know things that would be useful to the Resistance?"

"We do," said Jan in surprise.

"Right. When Major Konrad and the other Nazis come to my house, they tell my father all sorts of things."

"Yes!" cried Jan. "And my father often tells my mother what the German plans are. But, Elli, we can't tell these things to the Resistance because they would not believe or trust us. Who can we tell?"

"We'll have to figure that out," said Elli.

Just then, they saw an empty, old hut behind some trees. The door was hanging open, and the roof had fallen in. They stopped and stared.

"Did you know there was an empty hut here in the woods?" said Jan.

Elli shook her head. "It's not empty at all. Look! Someone is coming out."

CHAPTER 5

IN HIDING

Jan and Elli hid behind a tree and watched. A man and a girl came out. They were very thin, and their clothes were torn and old. They were picking things up off the ground.

"They're looking for mushrooms," said Jan.

As they got nearer, Jan took a sharp breath. Elli looked at him but said nothing.

As soon as the two were out of sight, Elli asked, "Who are they? Do you know them?"

"It's Dr. Stein, our dentist, and his daughter, Ruth, who was in our class."

"I didn't live here then," Elli said. "Are they Jews?"

Jan nodded, "Yes. People said they had moved to England or America."

"There will be a reward for anyone who tells the Germans where they are. The Nazi Police offer lots of money to people who betray Jews."

"Elli, what are you thinking?"

"No! I'm not going to betray them. But more and more people come here now to look for food and wood. The Steins will be discovered."

Just then, they heard the sound of voices and hid behind some bushes.

"Dr. Stein, you mustn't go out into the woods. It's not safe," said a voice they knew. "I got you some milk and fish and a little bread. It's not much, but it's the best I can do. We're all going hungry now."

Jan began to shake. It was Pieter, the boy who bullied him. Pieter's father had been shot for being in the Resistance. Now Pieter was risking his own life by hiding and feeding Jews.

"You're right, Pieter," said Dr. Stein. "But we need some fresh air, and mushrooms and roots to eat."

"But you can't risk your life and Ruth's, too. The war will end soon. The British and Americans are in France. Just wait a little longer."

"We're very grateful to you, Pieter. But we can't stand living in this old hut much longer," said Ruth.

"Look. I've got some books for you," Pieter told her. "And here's a pack of cards. It's the best I can do."

"Stay here until it gets dark," said Pieter. "Then go to the Groots' farm. There you can warm up and get some hot food."

"And take a bath?" asked Ruth with a smile.

"There's no hot water anymore," Pieter told her.

"It gets worse and worse," said Ruth.

"I know," grinned Pieter. "But the war's nearly over now."

"People have been saying that for months." Ruth shook her head.

"Yes, but this time it's true," said her father. "Look at the British and American planes that fly overhead. They're bombing Germany. Soon the Nazis will give up."

CHAPTER 6

RESISTANCE

Jan sat in the kitchen and ate his carrot and potato soup.

"It's the best I can do," said his mother. "You can't get meat or bread anywhere. Just be grateful it's hot. When our coal runs out, you'll be eating cold food."

Just then, Jan heard the sound of an axe. He ran to the window and saw his father in the garden, cutting down their apple tree.

"Dad, no!" he yelled. "I love that tree! I used to swing on it when I was little. And we can eat the apples."

"It's too bad," his father yelled back. "But we need to keep warm. You can't get upset about a tree these days. Come and help me. Major Konrad will be here soon."

"I'll just finish my soup," called Jan. He ate it as slowly as he could. Soon he heard the sound of a motorbike, and Major Konrad strode in.

Jan's father came in from outside.

"We need you, Bakker," said the major. "We've been told that there are young men hiding in the woods near the old hut. They could be Resistance fighters or Jews. Meet us at midnight. We need all the men we can get."

Jan began to hum as if he hadn't heard anything.

"See you at midnight, Major. Heil Hitler!" cried Jan's father.

"Heil Hitler!" replied the major.

Jan was thinking fast. "Mom, I feel sick. I can't help Dad with the tree right now."

"All right, Jan," said his mother. She put a hand on his head. "You do feel hot. You'd better lie down for a while."

Jan let his mother tuck him in bed.

As soon as she left his room, he grabbed a scrap of paper and wrote:

> *They are going to search the woods*
> *near you today. Go and hide*
> *on the other side of the river.*
>
> *A friend*

Then he got up, climbed out of his window, and ran to the woods. When Jan got near the old hut, he hid behind a tree. He picked up a stone.

He wrapped the note around the stone and threw it at the window. The glass smashed.

They must have heard it, Jan thought, and he turned around and ran home before anyone saw him.

Jan climbed back into his room through the window. His heart was thumping. Will they find the note? he wondered. Did I get there in time?

When his mother came up with more soup on a tray, he told her he was feeling better.

"I'd rather eat at the table," he said. Then he would hear any news.

Jan sat in the kitchen all day, waiting for news. He was scared.

At last his father came in and slammed the door. They didn't find them, thought Jan, or he'd be in a better mood.

"You were hunting people like animals," his wife told him. "You should be ashamed."

"They're not people. Jews and Resistance fighters are rats," he replied. "Anyway, we didn't find anyone. But someone had been living in the hut. There were still the remains of a fire and food in there."

"Maybe someone warned them," said Jan's mother.

"No," said his father. "Only the Germans and the Police knew we were going to search the woods."

Jan was listening carefully.

"Anyway, whoever was in that old hut has escaped for now," said his father.

CHAPTER 7

ELLI

On the way to school the next day, Jan saw Elli. He ran to catch up with her. "Hey, Elli, I did it," he told her, smiling.

"What did you do?" Elli asked.

"I was in the kitchen yesterday when Major Konrad came to tell my dad that they were going to search the woods. I went and told the Steins."

Elli stopped and looked at him with huge eyes. "You told them?"

Jan nodded.

"I wrote a note. I didn't say it was from me. I wrapped it around a stone and tossed it through the window."

"Jan, that was so clever. I'm so proud of you."

"Look at the lovebirds," came Pieter's voice.

"Jan loves Elli, Jan loves Elli," Pieter's buddies sang.

"Don't listen to them," Elli told Jan. But she blushed a deep red. Then she took his arm. Jan saw that she held her head high for the first time that he could remember.

"We need a plan. Let's meet after school," said Elli.

So after school, Jan planned to go over to Elli's house.

"Be back before dark," said his mother. "We don't want the Nazis to arrest you for being out late."

"You're a bit young to be going out with girls, aren't you?" said his father.

"Don't tease him. He needs friends," said Mrs. Bakker. "It's hard on Jan and me to be hated by everyone because you're a Nazi-lover. No one will talk to us. Elli is the only friend Jan has at the moment, so leave him alone."

Jan smiled at his mother and ran out the door.

Jan didn't notice a gang of boys coming toward him. One of them put out his foot and tripped him.

He fell flat on his face. The other boys laughed as Jan got to his feet and limped to Elli's house.

When Jan got there, Elli took him up to the bathroom and washed the blood off his hands and face.

"I wish it was all over, Elli," said Jan. "It just goes on and on."

"But, Jan, don't you see? It's good. Now that you've begun to make use of what you hear at home, the Nazis might suspect us. But if we are still being bullied, no one will think that we've changed sides."

"You're so clever, Elli," said Jan. "Have you heard anything new today?"

Elli shook her head, "No, nothing. The Nazis are very angry because they searched the woods all day and found no one. They have no new plans at the moment."

"I think the Germans know that things are going badly for them. The British or American soldiers will be here in a few weeks or months."

"I know," agreed Elli. "But we must try to make sure that no one else gets killed before they get here."

"We're part of the Resistance, aren't we, Elli?" smiled Jan. "In our own way."

"We are," she smiled back. "We are. There's only two of us, but we're playing a very important part."

CHAPTER 8

HUNGER

Jan's family sat close to their tiny log fire. The cooking pot hung over it. They were all wrapped up in blankets. They had no gas, no electricity, and very little coal or food.

"Your friends, the Germans, keep punishing us all the time," said Jan's mother. "We have so little food that some people are slowly starving."

"Don't start that again," replied her husband.

"At least we still have something to eat," Jan's mother said, as she handed him a bowl with a few potatoes. There was something else floating in the water.

"What's this, Mom?" asked Jan.

"Your mother is giving us tulip bulbs to eat," said his father. "That's all we can find."

Jan made himself eat the soup. It was awful.

Just then a German named Private Stern came in with a very young soldier. "Sorry to bother you, Bakker, but the major wants you at Nazi Head Office."

Jan hoped he could find out what was going on.

"Is it something important?" he asked Private Stern.

"No, Jan, they're just arresting some more people."

Then he turned to Jan's mother. "I am sorry, but we have orders to search every house. We are looking for Resistance fighters, and for young men who are hiding to avoid being sent to work camps," said Private Stern.

"But my husband is in the Nazi Police. You can't suspect us of hiding anyone," said Jan's mother.

"My orders are to search every house in town. Even stupid orders have to be carried out."

"Go on then. We have nothing to hide," she replied.

While the soldiers were searching, Jan raced over to Elli's house.

"Elli, the Germans are searching every house in town!"

"We know who's working against the Germans," cried Elli. "We'll push notes under their doors to warn them and then ring the bell and run."

"And no one will know it was us," said Jan.

As fast as they could, Jan and Elli wrote the notes. They slipped them under doors, rang doorbells, and then ran away as they had planned.

CHAPTER 9

SUSPICION

Spring came, and it got warmer. But still there was very little food. Everyone looked thin and sick.

Sometimes the Germans gave Jan's father a package of meat. It was cooked in a thick soup with potatoes and carrots and had to last for days.

Major Konrad came to eat with them one evening, bringing some oranges as a gift.

I hate
doing this.

Jan decided he hated Major Konrad
so much he wouldn't eat an orange.

"Yes, you Dutch are being very difficult," Major Konrad said, "and there is a traitor among you. We must find him and punish him."

"What do you mean?" asked Jan's father.

"You know, Bakker. Every time we try to find the Resistance fighters and the Jews, they're gone. Someone is warning them."

Jan was scared. "Do you know who's warning them?" he asked.

"I think so," replied the major. "Have an orange, Jan, they're good."

Shaking, Jan took an orange. If the major thought he was the traitor, it was not a good idea to refuse his gift.

As soon as he could, Jan rushed over to Elli's house.

"Major Konrad knows that people are being warned when a search is coming," he told her. "He says he thinks he knows who it is."

"Does he think it's you?" asked Elli.

"I think so," nodded Jan.

"You must be careful. I'll deliver the notes alone from now on."

"They might suspect you, too," Jan pointed out. "The risk is the same for both of us."

"No, it isn't," said Elli. "I'm a girl, and everyone in this town thinks I'm a wimp. But I heard my father talking on the phone today, and there is something we have to do at once."

"What?" demanded Jan.

"We have to go and warn Pieter."

"The Nazi Police are coming to arrest him today," she said. "They know he's part of the Resistance."

"Good!" said Jan. "I hate Pieter. He's made my life miserable for years. I'm not going to risk my life for him." And he went toward the door.

Elli stood between Jan and the door. "Jan, stop it!" she yelled. "You sound like a Nazi! Just remember, we're on the side of the Resistance."

"But, Elli," said Jan. "Pieter has bullied you, too. How can you care what happens to him?"

"Because he's a human being. Of course he's angry with the Germans. His father was shot, remember? Of course he hates us. He thinks we're on the same side as his father's killers."

Jan blushed. "You're right, Elli. But it's very hard to care about people who hate you."

"I know," said Elli. "Now, you write the note, and I'll go out and toss it through Pieter's window."

Jan wrote in capital letters:

GET OUT! THE POLICE
ARE COMING FOR YOU
TONIGHT!

"Good," said Elli. "Now give it to me and go home." Elli ran down the street with the note in her pocket.

Jan set out for home. Then he thought to himself, I must make sure she's all right. I'll follow her.

Jan followed Elli through the empty streets until they came to Pieter's house.

Jan could see Pieter's mother through the window.

Elli picked up a stone, wrapped the note around it, and threw it at the window, which broke.

But to his horror, Jan saw that the note had dropped off and was blown across the street. Jan ran to fetch it. He tore it into tiny pieces.

Just then the door of the house flew open, and Pieter's mother rushed out. Elli ran, but the woman was too fast for her and grabbed her.

"You little Nazi-lover," she shouted. "Smashing people's windows!"

Jan ran up. "It's all my fault," he told the angry woman. "I told her to do it. Your Pieter has made us both miserable for too long."

"I'm glad the Nazis are coming for him today," he added.

Pieter's mother turned pale. She ran back into the house.

"Well, we gave her the message," said Elli, smiling.

"Yes, but we're in a mess now," Jan replied.

CHAPTER 10

ARRESTED

Elli and Jan walked back to Jan's house. Jan's mother was at the door waiting for them, in tears.

"How could you two do that?" she shouted. "People hate us anyway. This war will be over any day now, and we've been on the wrong side."

Elli and Jan looked at each other. They knew that they hadn't been on the wrong side.

"Why did you smash that window?" Jan's mother went on.

"It wasn't Jan. It was me," Elli told her.

"But I told her to do it," added Jan.

Just then, there was a knock at the door. It was Private Stern.

"Sorry, Mrs. Bakker, but I've been told to bring these two children into Nazi Head Office. There are a few questions we need to ask them. In fact, they've done something very bad."

"What — smashed a window?"

"We have to keep order. Come on, Elli and Jan, this won't take long."

As the three of them walked to the Police Station, Jan asked, "What's going to happen to us?"

"You'll have to wait and see," he replied. "Now listen, you two. I know what you've been up to, and I don't blame you. I'd have done the same myself. This awful war is almost over. It will only be a few days now. There's no point in more killing. So just say you're sorry. Tell them you didn't mean to do it. Then go home and stay there until it's all over. Don't try to be heroes, okay?"

"Why are you helping us?" asked Elli. "We're not on the same side."

"Oh yes, we are," said Private Stern. "We're longing for this war to be over. Now, don't say anything, and I won't betray you. Let's all pray to God that it's over soon."

Elli and Jan stared at Private Stern.

"Don't be surprised. Not all Germans are monsters," said the private. "I have never agreed with Hitler, nor with the Nazi Party. But Major Konrad's a real Nazi, so just be very polite. Tell him how sorry you are, and pretend to be scared."

"I am scared," Jan told him.

"Good," nodded Private Stern as they arrived at the Nazi Head Office. "Now remember what I said, and don't try to be heroes."

CHAPTER 11

HITLER'S DEAD

Jan and Elli sat outside Major Konrad's room for a long time.

"He always does this," Jan told Elli. "Dad told me he does it just to make people even more scared."

"Well it works, doesn't it?" said Elli. "I'm shaking all over."

Then the door opened and there stood Major Konrad looking very angry. "All right, you two. You come in first, Miss Elli."

"Thank you, Major Konrad," said Elli, and she walked into the room. The door slammed behind her.

Jan felt sick. He could hear Major Konrad shouting. Is this just about a broken window, thought Jan, or does Major Konrad really know something?

At last, Elli was pushed out of the room. Jan could see she had been crying. Then Major Konrad yelled, "All right, Jan Bakker, your turn."

Jan stood with his head down, trying to look sorry.

"Yes," said Major Konrad, "I know it all. You and Elli have been warning Jews and Resistance fighters. You told them when we were going to conduct a search. That's how they got away."

Jan thought, Major Konrad is just saying this. He knows nothing. Elli would never tell him anything.

"Oh, no," cried Jan. "Why would Elli and I do that? After all, our families are on your side."

"Well, the war won't last forever. You may be afraid you backed the wrong side. You may want to make sure you won't be punished when we go back to Germany and leave you to face the Resistance."

Jan saw that Major Konrad didn't know the truth.

"Oh, no, Major, I don't feel like that at all! I mean, my father has been working for you all through the war."

"Besides," he added. "No one in the Resistance would believe a word we said."

"That makes sense," said the major. "Someone tipped off the Jews hiding in the hut. And someone told everyone that we were coming to search people's houses. If it's not you and Elli, then who is it?"

"I don't know, Major," said Jan. "But I hope you find them soon."

"I will, don't worry. Now, off you go, and don't smash any more windows. I don't want Pieter's mother in here again. She's no friend of yours, I can tell you."

"No, sir. I hate Pieter. He picks on Elli and me all the time. We wish you'd put him in prison, sir."

"Good. Well, off you go now."

Shaking all over, Jan left the major's office. He passed a room where some soldiers were listening to the radio. Jan stopped for a moment and heard a voice saying, "Our great leader, Adolf Hitler, is dead. He died doing his duty. Long live Germany . . ."

Jan saw that many of the soldiers were crying.

Yippee! The war is almost over, thought Jan, as he raced out into the street to find Elli and tell her the wonderful news.

CHAPTER 12

THE TRUTH IS TOLD

One moment the town was silent and then, a second later, everyone seemed to spill out into the streets.

"The Germans have lost the war!" they were shouting.

"The war is over!"

"The British are almost here!"

"Peace at last!"

That night, a huge bonfire was lit in the town, and the town band played. People danced and sang.

In Jan's small room, Jan and Elli listened to the music and smelled the sweet aroma from the bonfire.

"Come on, Jan," cried Elli. "Let's dance, just the two of us."

Suddenly, the music stopped.

"What is it?" asked Elli. They looked out the window.

"Listen. Tanks!" cried Jan. "I can hear them."

"Are the Germans coming back?" asked Elli, feeling scared.

"No, it's the British!"

"Look, there's Pieter," said Jan.

"He's sitting up on one of the tanks. They're British tanks! The British are here to set us free!" shouted Jan.

"Oh, Jan," said Elli, "this is the best moment of my life!"

"Mine, too," agreed Jan. "But remember, to everyone else, we're still the children of Nazi-lovers. They'll still hate us."

"I don't care," said Elli. "I know, and you know, that we did our best to help the Resistance."

Then there was a loud knock at the door.

"It's the Dutch Police," Jan said.

"They must have come for your father," Elli replied.

"Jan," came his mother's voice. "Come down at once."

Jan ran downstairs. His mother's face was pale, and she was crying. "They've come to take away your father. Say goodbye to him."

Jan looked at his father, wearing handcuffs and looking scared.

"Goodbye, Dad. Come back soon," he said and tried hard to smile.

"Bye, son. Take care of your mother. Do your best. I'll be thinking of you."

"Enough of that, Bakker," said a police officer. "Think about all the men you handed over to the Germans. What happened to *their* wives and children? Now, move on, you creep. Prison's too good for you."

Jan could see how much the officer hated his father. He knew he would not see his dad again for a long time.

* * *

Life went on the same for Jan and Elli. No one would speak to them at school. Only Ruth, the daughter of the Jewish dentist, was kind.

"It's not Elli's or Jan's fault that their fathers were Nazi-lovers," she told the other children, "just as it wasn't my fault that my father was a Jew." But no one listened to her.

Then the news got around that Ruth and her family were going to leave to start a new life in America.

"Let's send her a good luck card," said Jan. "She's been so nice to us."

"Good idea," agreed Elli.

So Elli made a card and Jan wrote:

To our friend Ruth, the only
one who tried to understand.
Good luck!

They went down to the train station to give it to her.

The whole town was at the train station to say goodbye to the Steins. Jan and Elli had to push their way through the crowd to get to Ruth. Jan handed her the card. She opened it and a look of surprise came over her face.

"Jan," she said. "Jan Bakker, I've seen this writing before. It was you who warned us that the Germans were going to search the woods. It was you! It was, wasn't it?"

Jan blushed.

"Was it you?" demanded Ruth and Dr. Stein.

"Yes, it was Jan," shouted Elli. "He risked his life for you and lots of others."

"Not just me," said Jan, "Elli did, too. It was Elli who threw the stone through your window, Pieter."

"You were trying to warn us?" asked Pieter in amazement.

"We *did* warn you," said Elli.

"Let's get this straight. Are you saying that you found out about the German plans from your fathers and then warned us?" asked Pieter.

Jan and Elli nodded.

The train began to move.

"Jan and Elli, thank you, and God bless you," shouted Ruth from a window as the train gathered speed. "You were heroes. You saved our lives!"

For a moment there was a silence in the crowd.

Then Pieter said, "Jan, Elli, would you like to come and have some coffee with me? I want to hear more."

"We'd love to, thank you," they said.

"I think we should thank you for what you did for the Resistance," said Pieter. "We have treated you badly. Maybe now we can start to make up for it."

Pieter put his arm around Jan's shoulders. "We may even end up being friends again."

Then the three of them ran off together, laughing, to catch up with the rest of their classmates.

ABOUT THE AUTHOR

Ann Jungman grew up as the daughter of German Jewish refugees, so she knows a lot about World War II and the Nazis.

Ann became a teacher and loved reading to her students. She began making up her own stories, and the kids loved them so much that she wrote them down.

Ann now lives in London and is a full-time writer.

GLOSSARY

aroma (uh-ROH-muh)—a pleasant smell

betray (bi-TRAY)—to be disloyal or unfaithful

canal (kuh-NAL)—a long, narrow strip of water

Nazi Party (NOT-zee PAR-tee)—the political group run by Adolf Hitler that controlled Germany from 1933 to 1945; the Nazi Party believed that Germans were better than other races of people, such as Jews; the Nazi Party fought World War II to try to spread its beliefs around the world.

resistance (ri-ZISS-tuhnss)—a secret group that opposes the ruling government

salute (sah-LOOT)—to give a sign of respect or honor

traitor (TRAY-tur)—a person who helps the enemies of his country

DISCUSSION QUESTIONS

1. Jan and Elli betrayed their fathers by helping the Dutch people who were under German rule. Do you think it was okay that they went against their fathers' wishes? Why or why not?

2. Jan's dad was arrested by the British at the end of the war. Jan knew he wouldn't see his dad for a long time. How do you think Jan felt about his father going to prison?

3. Jan's father went against his own people and worked for the Germans. Why do you think he did this? What price did his family pay for his decision?

WRITING PROMPTS

1. Jan and Elli were almost caught for helping the Resistance. Write about what would have happened to them if they had been caught.

2. Pieter and the other kids hated Jan and Elli, and mistreated them because of what their fathers did. Write about a time you were blamed or mistreated because of what someone else said or did.

3. Jan and Elli helped Pieter even though he was cruel to them. Have you ever helped someone who was mean to you? Write about what you did. Why did you help that person?

INTERNET SITES

Do you want to know more about subjects related to this book? Or are you interested in learning about other topics? Then check out FactHound, a fun, easy way to find Internet sites.

Our investigative staff has already sniffed out great sites for you!

Here's how to use FactHound:

1. Visit *www.facthound.com*

2. Select your grade level.

3. To learn more about subjects related to this book, type in the book's ISBN number: **1598890018**.

4. Click the **Fetch It** button.

FactHound will fetch the best Internet sites for you!